D0666980

NO LONGER PROPERTY
OF ANYTHINK
RANGEVIEW LIBRARY
DISTRICT

THE ARRANGEMENT

VOL. 3

H.M. Ward

www.SexyAwesomeBooks.com

Laree Bailey Press

This book is a work of fiction. Names, characters, places, and incidents are either the product of the author's imagination or are used fictitiously, and any resemblance to actual persons, living or dead, events, or locales is entirely coincidental.

Copyright © 2013 by H.M. Ward
All rights reserved.

No part of this book may be reproduced, scanned, or distributed in any printed or electronic form.

Laree Bailey Press
First Print Edition: May 2013

THE ARRANGEMENT

VOL. 3

CHAPTER 1

Breathing hard, I watch the door slip shut. Shock washes over me. I don't know what I expected things to be like, but this isn't it. Wide-eyed, I pad over to the bed and sit down. The sheets are rumpled. The room smells like Sean and sex. I can't think. I can't breathe. The sensation worsens, growing tighter and tighter until I'm gasping for air.

Tears streak my face as I throw myself onto a pillow. I grip it and try to suck in air, but I can't. Sean's scent hits me hard and makes me choke. I push myself up and try to get hold of my emotions. I knew this wasn't real. It's all a game. Sean is fucked up and he needs things this way. There is a reason for it. He said that over and over again, but it doesn't mesh. Nothing does. It's like there are two different versions of him. One is playful and kind. The other is so messed up that he can't fuck a girl he hasn't paid for. I clutch my face and push the tears away with the back of my hand. I've fallen for him. I can't help it.

I want to call Mel, but she's working. I need to get control over my feelings. I need to. I have to. Suddenly, the urge to go for a run hits me hard. Fresh air, the night wind in my face—all that shit will clear my head. I just need to get out of here. I glance at my ankle, wondering what Miss Black will do if I leave the building.

Screw that. I need this.

Padding to the closet, I yank the door, but it doesn't open. I pull it again, but it doesn't move. My vision is blurry from tears. I lean over and look at the handles. They lock. Sean locked the closet before he left. Rage flashes through, me so hot and hard that I can't stand it. My arm swings on its own and smashes into the door. I scream, but it doesn't make me feel better.

Wearing nothing but a robe, I turn and lean against the closet doors. I slide to the floor and hold my face in my hands. Every second I stay in this room, I feel the walls closing in around me. There's no air. I'm trapped. I tug at my hair, angry. I love him. How could I be so stupid? I close my eyes and sit there until the panic recedes. I can leave the room, but I have no clothes. I won't get very far. The hotel staff will stop me before the elevator reaches the ground floor.

My phone rings. It takes me a second to recognize the ringtone. It's Mel. I dart across the room, grabbing my purse and dumping it out on the floor. I answer just before voicemail picks up. "Mel!"

"Avery girl, are you all right? Shit, you don't sound all right. Say something. Let me hear you talk." Mel shushes someone in the background.

My voice is shaky. "I thought you were at work."

"I was. I'm done. Guy was working on speedy issues." Someone starts laughing in the background.

I recognize that chuckle. "Is that Marty?" Why are they hanging out together? They hate each other.

"Yeah, honey. Now tell me what that piece of shit did to you. Are you hurt? I'll kick his white ass myself—"

I cut her off. "No, I'm not hurt. He got mad and left. I wanted to go after him," I lie. I can't tell her that I was going to leave the building. "But he locked the closet. I can't get my clothes."

"What'd she say?" I hear Marty asking in the background.

"Shut your face, Showboat. I'll tell you later," Mel snaps at Marty. Then she says to me, "This is easy. Go look at the door." I walk over there, unsure of what she wants me to do. "What kind is it? Single door? Double doors?"

"Double. They close in the center. There's no doorjamb down the middle. The handle is the lever kind."

"Yeah, cuz that matters," she says sarcastically. "Haven't you ever busted into a room before?"

I stare at the phone like that's the stupidest question ever. When I put it back to my ear, I say, "My roommate locks me out on a regular basis. What do you think?"

"Don't get fresh with me. I don't like to put my nose in other people's business. How was I...?" Marty is cracking up in the background. He's mocking her because Mel is always in everybody's business. When she speaks again, her tone is terse. She doesn't comment on Marty's giggles. "Okay, Avery, this one is easy. Look between the doors, down by the lock. If you're lucky, the lock is in there backwards and you just have to shove a credit card through the middle. If not, you have to work it in from behind."

"How do I know which way will work?" I look at it, not sure what I'm supposed to see.

"The locking part is flat. If it's in backwards, the part facing you is curved. What do you see?"

Peering through the slat in the door, I can see a gold piece of metal. "It's curved."

"Good. Pop that baby open." Mel waits while I dig through my purse and grab my debit card. I push it into the space between the two doors and it slips right in. I pull the door and it opens.

"It worked!" I say surprised. I glance at the card. Damn. That was easy.

"Of course it worked. You think I don't know stuff? Well, I do."

Marty sings in the background, "She does!"

"Shut up, Showtunes," Mel snaps at Marty. "Listen Avery, if that messed up fucker hurts you, crush the button on your bracelet."

"It's not like that," I say, as I look through the closet for my dress. Sean's coat is hanging up next to my dress. I bump the hanger and his coat falls to the floor. Something falls out of the pocket. I pick it up and look at a crumpled ball of paper. "Listen, thanks for helping. I should be home for a little bit tomorrow. I'll catch up with you guys then." I hang up the phone.

Something about the paper seems weird. Sean has this really nice coat, but has garbage in the pockets? I think it's strange, so I stick my hands into both pockets. They're empty. I didn't think he was the kind of guy to shove nasty old stuff in his coat. He's too highbrow for that.

I look at the balled up paper again and open it. In that moment, everything changes. I stare blankly at the note, not fathoming the depths of what's happening. People are like this. People do one thing and say another. It fits with Sean's words when he walked out. He thought he could do it, but he can't. Not this time. Something changed. Something's different, and now I know what it is.

I stare at the paper, reading the pretty cursive letters over and over again.

We love you! —Amanda & Baby

CHAPTER 2

I can't swallow. I stare at the paper, feeling my throat grow tighter and tighter. There's a baby. He's a father. Sean is married and has a baby. Oh, holy…

I sit down hard and stare at the note. It was written hastily on a piece of computer paper. There are smudge marks, like someone grabbed it—the baby maybe. This is what he couldn't say. It had nothing to do with me. It's him. I press my eyes closed. I don't know what to do. He has a family and he's cheating—with me.

Misery bubbles up inside my chest. I wad the paper back up and put it in his pocket so it looks like I never saw it. I lock the closet door and make sure everything is back the way it was. Then, I walk into the bathroom and turn on the shower. I drop the robe to the floor and step in. I stand there, letting the water wash away every ounce of remorse I have. Sean's a dick. He's not what I thought at all. I wonder if I should confront him. It sounds insane, but I feel like I'm the one being cheated on.

He's not yours, Avery, a little voice says in the back of my mind. *He never was.*

This is a job. That's what it's always been to him. That's what it always will be. I swallow hard and turn off the water. After I towel off, I grab my phone and call Black.

"How are things going?" she says with her silky voice.

"Very well. I'd like to throw my name in for more work as soon as this is over." Even as I said the words, I can't believe I'm saying them. If Sean is like this, if I have to finish this job, by the time I'm done I'm going to be so emotionally repressed that it won't matter who I fuck. Maybe this is what

Mel and Black meant. Maybe it's the reason why they ended up staying and taking more clients.

"Excellent, Avery." Her voice has that hollow politeness that irritates me. I hear it now, vibrating like a plucked string. "Let me make sure I understand you correctly. You don't want any time off between clients?"

"No," I say, "The sooner the better."

"I understand. Is there anything else?"

Is there? Should I tell her that I'm disillusioned? Should I tell her that I fell for Sean, but he's just a cheating jackass? I smile to myself. I sound like an idiot. "No, that's all."

I press END CALL and toss my phone back in my bag. I let the numbness overtake me. There's no other way to get through this, and I have to finish it. There's no other way to survive.

———

I leave the room in nothing but my robe around 2:00am. I'm stopped on the ground floor by the hotel manager. He's an older, squat man wearing a pristine black suit. It distracts from his round face.

"Miss Ferro," he says, taking my elbow to keep me from walking through the lobby. "May I help you with something?"

I nod. "Is Sean down here somewhere? I didn't see him at the bar."

"Yes, he is. Let me take you to him." I walk next to the man. He offers, "My name is Thomas. If you need anything, I'm happy to help. Mr. Ferro is one of our best customers and as such, we try to humor his requests. However, I would appreciate it if you wore clothes next time you came down to the lobby."

My face flames red. "Oh, I'm sorry."

"It's a perfectly honest mistake," he smiles at me, but his eyes say he knows why I'm here, what I am. We stop in front of a set of huge double doors. Thomas pulls one open and says, "Good evening, Miss Ferro."

I step through the door and stop. Blinking rapidly, I try to get my eyes to adjust to the light. I glance around at an empty ballroom. There's a grand piano in the opposite corner. Sean is sitting in front of it, playing. I don't move. For a moment, I just watch him play. Sean's eyes are closed and his dark hair hangs down over his brow.

His body moves to the music like they're one and the same. The song is so somber, so dark. It tugs at my heart. I have to remind myself what Sean is, what he's done. But as I watch him play, I don't want to. I can't think about it. I don't have that luxury. I have to do this to survive. Sean's life is his to mess up. I tell myself that If Sean wants to sleep with hookers instead of his wife that it's none of my business, but I'm not that cold. I hate the idea of being the other woman, the girl that ruins a family. But that's what I am, a plaything with a high price tag.

Slowly, I pad across the room. The cold tiles chill my bare feet. Sean is still playing the lament when I come up behind him. It's a song I know well. I slip onto the bench and place my fingers on the keys. Sean glances at me, but he doesn't stop playing. I move my fingers with his, playing with him. Our shoulders brush together occasionally as I reach in front of him to press a key. Sean's blue gaze cuts to the side. He watches me as he plays. Neither of us says anything. When the song ends we both sit there, staring straight ahead.

"I'm sorry," Sean says. "I shouldn't have walked away like that."

I find a way to act like it didn't matter. I pretend that I don't know his secret. "You don't have to explain anything to me. It's fine, Sean."

His blue eyes slip over me. Sean hesitates before saying, "You play very well. Who taught you?"

"My mother." *I feel nothing.* If I keep thinking it, it'll happen. Eventually I'll feel nothing. Eventually, every last part of me will go numb. I won't react to his voice or his touch. I can do this. I stare straight ahead.

"She must be a wonderful musician."

I know he's searching for kind words, but I don't care. I answer bluntly. "She was. She died along with my father in a car wreck last year. That was my favorite song. I bugged her to help me with it frequently over the past few years."

Sean watches me as I speak. Finally, he says, "You've been through a lot." It's a statement. He leaves it hanging in the air, so I nod.

"Yeah, but who hasn't?" I try to sound apathetic, but I don't pull it off. I shrug and add, "What doesn't kill you makes you stronger, or so I hear." I glance at him, expecting him to make light of it, but he just nods.

"That's what I hear, too." After a moment, he says, "What other songs do you know?"

I look at the piano in front of me. A million memories of me and my mom flash by. She loved playing classical music. I preferred darker things, more contemporary stuff. I touch the keys lightly and start playing. To my surprise, Sean joins in. Neither of us speaks. We play like that, alternating songs until sleep pulls at me so hard that I can't keep my head up.

My fingers fumble a few times and Sean stops. He turns to me and stands. Leaning over, he scoops me up and cradles me in his arms. "Avery, I'm sorry if I hurt you." He sets me down, looking into my eyes. Sean presses his lips gently to mine and a surge of guilt nearly strangles me. I do everything I can manage to kiss him back and not act like his cheating bothers me, but it does.

That night I barely sleep. I keep seeing a beautiful woman holding a sweet baby in her arms. They're just faces, only something my mind dreamed up while I slept, but I feel like I stabbed them in the back. I'm not cut out for this. I wish I was dead inside. I wish I lost the ability to feel anything. I fall asleep thinking, wishing that I was someone else.

CHAPTER 3

The next morning, Sean is gone. He slipped out without waking me. There's a note on his pillow. I open it, and think of that crumpled piece of paper in his pocket. My heart clenches. I can't breathe. Pressing my eyes closed, I chase away the pain. Inhaling slowly, I open his note.

> *I'm sorry about last night. I didn't mean for things to go that way. I hope you'll take this morning off and return tonight in*

time for dinner. There are some more things I'll show you later. See you then.

-Sean

I dress quickly and call Miss Black to tell her that Sean set me free for daylight hours. She wants me to stay put, but Sean wanted me to go out. Eventually, Miss Black folds and I leave the hotel. When I finally get back to the dorm, I can't think straight. I want to scream. I want to bury my face in my pillow and cry. The thoughts rise up and choke me so hard that I can't swallow. It's been months since I felt this crazy.

I shove the key into my door and kick it open. The door slams open wide. When I glance up, I see Amber's brain-dead boyfriend—the exhibitionist—carving a turkey on my make-up counter. Turkey juices puddle around my blushes and drip onto the floor. He smiles broadly.

"Put some pants on!" I yell at him as I run into the room.

I left the door to the hallway open. The naked jackass waves to people as they pass by. Amber isn't even here and this idiot is eating turkey on my make-up counter. I can't deal with it. I feel my heart dying inside of me. I grab a pair of sweats and change in the bathroom.

When I emerge, naked guy mutters something about joining him, but I flip him off and run out the door.

I need to get out of here. As I run down the hall, Mel sticks her head out the door. "Hey bitch! Where you running off to? I thought you were…" When I don't stop, Mel steps out into the hallway. "Avery!" She calls after me, but I don't stop. I can't stop.

It takes a minute to start my car and I'm off. I don't plan to go there. I just go wherever this crushing feeling in my chest leads me. Staring through the grime on the windshield, I drive further east. A few turns and I pull up at the black iron gates that surround the cemetery. I managed to get here without stalling. It's still early. No one is here. I drive past the rows of tombstones towards the newer plots in the back. There's an open grave, the mound of dirt is covered with green plastic grass. I drive past it and turn off the main road in the cemetery and drive to the end. I pull over. The car shudders and lurches before it stalls.

My hair hangs limp around my face. I shove open the door and walk swiftly toward them. There's a knot in my throat that I can't swallow no matter how hard I try. Tears prick my eyes, but they won't fall. My parent's plot is behind a massive oak tree. Its ancient base hides me from onlookers. I fall to my knees at the foot of my parent's grave and double over to stop the pain. My forehead rests against the cold hard ground. My teeth catch my lips and I bite and hold them between my teeth. Sucking in a rush of cold air, I sit up suddenly. My hair flies back, tossing some twigs with it. My heart hammers inside of me. It's the only thing that tells me that this hell is real. Everything else seems too wrong. I stare straight ahead, seeing their names chiseled in stone, but seeing nothing at all.

The wind lifts the ends of my hair off my shoulders. I have no idea how long I kneel here, but my legs have pins and needles. I shift my weight and sit on the ground and pull my knees into my chest. I breathe, because that's all I can do. My anger has faded over the months. I no longer come here to yell at them for abandoning me. This time I don't know why I'm here. I got in my car and this is where I ended up.

I reach for something I stashed in my pocket before running out of my dorm room. The metal feels cold against my skin. It's a little silver cross. My mother gave it to me when I turned sixteen. She said it was to remind me of what's important when things get rough. Things are worse than rough. I clutch the cross so tightly that the ends bite into my palm. Still, it doesn't stop me. Pain is something I understand. The rest of this, the senselessness of it all, eludes me.

I speak into the air. Somehow it feels normal. "What do I do, now? I didn't think my heart could break any more than it already has. The pieces still inside of me feel like broken glass. Every time I take a breath, they stab into me. It never ends..." I press my lips together and breathe.

I look down at the cross in my hand. That cross meant something to her. I wish it meant something to me, but it doesn't. All I see is a necklace. I have no faith. It died along with my parents. I string the cross around my neck and fasten the clasp. It lies against my heart. This is the closest thing I'll ever have to the comfort of hearing my Mom's voice and feeling her arms around me again. My fingers press the cross closer. I sit there, looking at nothing, barely thinking, and slowly rock myself.

Time passes. I have no idea how much, but my body has become still and cold. When a sharp breeze cuts past my cheek, I lift my face. The vacant gaze that I've had since I passed the iron gates comes into focus as I see a man in a long black coat. He stands with his shoulders hunched, looking at the roses in his hand. He stands there frozen for a long time. When he moves, he bends over and places the flowers on the ground on the grave in front of him. When he stands, he throws his head back and looks up at the sky.

I see his face. It's Sean. I don't know what I'm doing or what I want from him. I just see his pain and react. Weaving my way around countless graves, I come up behind him. My fingers clutch the cross around my neck like it can save me. My entire body has gone numb from the cold. I have no jacket. I want to feel the sting of the wind. I desperately need something to make sense.

Sean must feel my eyes on his back. He turns slowly. At first I think he's going to be mad, but his gaze sinks to the ground and he turns back to the tombstone at his feet. I walk up next to him and he asks, "What are you doing here?"

My voice comes out gravely when I speak, "Same reason as you, I suppose."

"Your parents?" he asks. His voice sounds deep and strained.

I nod, but Sean doesn't see me. I'm not sure if he sees anything. He stares straight ahead at the grave with such intensity that I can't look. "Yeah, I needed to talk to them. I have no idea if they can hear me, but I just needed to be here. I can't explain it." I'm quiet for a second and then add, "But talking to the dead seems to be a one-sided conversation. I ask them for help, but they can't help me anymore. I'm on my own."

Sean turns his grief-stricken face toward me. Our eyes lock and I see my own pain mirrored in his eyes, but there's something else there too—something more. The wind rustles his dark hair. Sean looks so lost, so vulnerable. After a moment, my eyes fall on the tombstone. I see the name. I stare at it like I don't understand. I expected this to be his parents, but it's not.

The name carved into the headstone is Amanda Ferro.

Sean turns back to the grave. I stare at the roses he's placed on the ground. "Amanda was my wife," he says. His voice sticks to the back of his throat, barely audible. Sean doesn't say anything else.

I stare, unblinking. He was married and now Amanda is gone. The woman who wrote the note in his pocket is dead. The grave is old. There's no freshly turned soil, no indications of a recent funeral. Her death must have been years ago. Sean was much younger then, barely twenty by the look of him. I glance at the headstone again. There's only one name. *Where's the baby?* The lump in my throat grows as I think about what might have happened to them, about what horrors Sean had to have seen to render him the person standing next to me.

Every time I think I know what's going on, everything falls apart. I feel the anger and disappointment fracture. That wall I forced up around my heart shatters as it falls away. I reach for Sean's gloved hand and weave our fingers together. Sean lets me. We both stand there, staring, saying nothing.

Sometimes there is nothing to say.

After a few moments, he turns to me glassy-eyed. Sean's jaw is tense, like he's ready to bite someone's head off. His eyes move over my sweats and then return to my face. The wind picks up my hair and throws it over my eyes and mouth. Before I can move my hand to push it back, Sean does it for me. His eyes meet mine and he stares. I can feel him struggling to come back from the dark places in the back of his mind. I see it in his eyes and I know he can see the darkness in mine.

Part of me wants to shut down and push him out. I can't take what life is throwing at me. The sick part of the whole thing is that there's a squeaky voice in the back of my head that won't let me just lie down and die. She never gives up, even when she's had her ass handed to her time and time again.

Sean looks down at my hand and then back at my face. His voice is soft, careful. "Take me to meet them." There's a question in his words, like I have the option to say no. We watch each other carefully. Finally, I nod. I pull him onto the path and we walk back to my parent's grave in silence.

When I stop in front of them, I say, "This is Sean." I smile sadly and squeeze his hand. Sean squeezes back. We both stare at the head stone for a moment and say nothing. Finally, I say, "My mom would have liked you. She would have said you were too skinny and tried to stuff an unreasonable about of food down your throat." The thought makes me smile. She was like that, always trying to fatten up my friends.

A ghost of a smile passes over his lips. "What about your Dad?"

I smile. "Oh, he'd hate your guts. I'm sure of it."

Sean looks surprised and seriously amused. "And why is that?"

"Because you have heartbreaker written all over you. Daddy would have seen you coming from a mile away. He would have told you that he'd break every bone in your body if you hurt me." I smile thinking about it. Daddy always said it teasingly when I brought a guy home, but there was a current of truth there. He wanted to keep me safe and that meant keeping my heart in one piece. Right now my heart has broken so badly that all that is remains is dust.

The smile slips off my lips. Sean watches me. He knows what I'm thinking. It's almost like he feels the weight of the memory the same way I do. I flick my eyes to the headstone. "They got blindsided that night. So did I."

"I know what you mean." His voice is somber, deep. He adds, "What doesn't kill you makes you stronger." Sean says my words back to me, but they seem to have new meaning, like the old adage is a lie and we're the only ones who know the truth.

I nod slowly. "The thing is—I'm not stronger. I feel like I'm half dead, barely hanging on. Most days, I go through the motions, hoping the next day will be better.

Then, some days bitch-slap me so hard that it feels like that night all over again." As I speak, I stare at nothing. I see nothing. The memories from that night flash through my mind. I shiver and shake it away, refusing to relive the horror again.

"And today was one of those days?" Sean says it so casually, but it's as if he knows the turmoil he caused me. I feel his eyes on the side of my face, but I don't look up. I just stare straight ahead. He sighs and looks past the tree toward his wife's grave. "Last night, something you did stirred up a memory. I couldn't repress it. That's why I left. I didn't mean to be cruel to you. I'd take it back if I could, Avery."

Sean's words should make me feel elated, but the heaviness is too great. His remorse, the pain in his voice strums through me and resonates. I know that feeling. Anything can conjure a memory—a song, a scent, a touch. I glance over at him. "I know you would."

There are more words to say, but neither of us says them. Death has fucked us both up to the point that we're barely functioning.

CHAPTER 4

Sean insists on getting me coffee. As we walk back to his car, he wraps his coat over my shoulders.

"Really, I'm fine. It's better this way." I try to shirk it off and give the wool coat back to him, but Sean puts it on me again, pressing my shoulders tight.

"No, it's not. Avery, there are other things to do—ways to feel something besides pain." Sean glances at me out of the corner of his eye. When we get to his car, he pulls the door open and holds it for me.

"What makes you think that's what I'm doing?" I stop in front of him. Sean's warm breath turns white as he sighs, looking down at me.

"Can you seriously ask me that question? Now you know why I avoid New York. Now you know why I'm a deranged fuck that can't get involved with anyone, the reason why I was looking for a call girl. When Amanda died, she left a hole in my chest. Not a day goes by, that I don't feel it pulling, trying to suck me under. Some days I let it. Some days I can't stand the thought of tomorrow, of going through the motions again." Sean speaks with confidence, but his eyes say something else. His hand is clutched into a tight fist. He holds it over his heart, protecting what's left.

The pit of my stomach falls away as he speaks. I know exactly what he's talking about. "So you hired me. That's how you deal with it?" His gaze falls to the side and he nods. A year ago, I would have condemned him for saying something like that, but not now. I've been through too much to judge him. Sean's protecting himself, forcing himself to feel something besides grief. It is the same thing that I do, leaving with no coat.

"So, your sweater and lack of coat might not stem entirely from money issues, am I right?" Sean presses his forehead to mine. A light smile crosses his lips.

I look up at him from under my lashes. "No one has noticed that before. I'm not even sure I knew what I was doing. I understand feeling cold. I understand what it means and what I should do. But, my God—Sean I don't understand this." I gesture at the grave yard. "I don't know what to do. Days pass and turn into months, but nothing changes. It's not better. I feel myself getting chipped away. Soon there will be nothing left to hold on to."

My throat tightens as I speak and I drop my gaze. It feels like someone is strangling me. Admitting that I don't know how to cope with all this makes me feel weak, like I'll falter and fade away. This entire time, I've carried this massive burden on my own two shoulders. I've never said it to anyone, and here I am confessing my deepest secret to the guy who bought me.

Sean pulls me against his chest and holds on tight. I can barely feel his touch, I'm so numb. He squeezes me tighter and tighter until all the air is forced out of my lungs. That's when he loosens his grip. "There is more to hold onto than you think." He kisses my forehead and releases me.

I'm aware of the warmth, of his moist lips on my cold skin, but I can't feel the kiss. It has no comfort, no joy. It's just a touch, like pressing my finger to the tip of a needle. I've done that, just to see if I could feel the sharp pain of the needle when it pricked my skin. Instead, the only indication that I should stop was a bead of blood that dripped down my palm.

Sean's voice pulls me from the memory. "Avery, let's not waste the day just trying to muddle through it. Let's do something." Sean smiles softly at me. "We'll start with coffee and go from there." I nod.

Sean holds the door to his shiny black sports car open and I slip into the seat. When Sean gets in and turns on the car, I ask, "No motorcycle?"

"I only ride when your car is in danger of being stolen and right now," he lifts his chin toward my car, "it looks like it's in its element." His voice is lighter, his tone teasing.

"Hey!" I smile at him and add, "Don't dis my car. She's been with me through thick and thin."

"I'll have her returned to your dorm while we're out so she can continue to attract scallywags and thieves." Sean starts the car and glances over at me with a playful look on his face.

I snort laugh, not expecting his lightness. "Scallywags?"

"Yes, and that would be me. The day we met, your little car attracted both types of very virtuous men." The corner of his mouth twitches, like he wants to smile.

"Yeah, normally I'd shove everyone in the backseat and cruise up and down Deer Park Avenue blasting the radio."

That makes him smile. He pulls away from the cemetery and for the first time in a long time, I feel like I might be okay.

CHAPTER 5

With a cup of hot coffee in hand, Sean drives without telling me where he's going. "Seriously," I ask. "You aren't even going to give me a hint?"

Sean glances at me out of the corner of his eye. "Nope."

"Well, you suck." He chuckles, but I talk over him. "Come on, just one little hint." The hot little cup warms my hands.

"You'll have to do better than that, Miss Smith." There's a faint smile on his lips. Sean drives for a while and after a few turns, we're at a toy store.

"Reliving your childhood, are we?" I say, arching an eyebrow at him.

"Perhaps," he says, noncommittally, and walks around to open my door. I'm not used to it. I already have my hand on the door, and push it open at the same time he steps in front of the door. The result is instant. The door smacks into his waist and forces out a gush of air the same way as if a fat guy slugged his chest.

I jump out of the car. "Oh my God! I'm sorry. Are you all right?" Sean holds his hand to his stomach and bends over. He straightens but I can tell that it hurts from the way his face is pinched.

"I'm fine," he says through his teeth and tries to smile. The way he looks, something about the way he says it, makes me laugh. Placing my hand on his shoulder, I mean to offer my apologies but I can't stop laughing. My emotions are so screwed up. They turn on in short uncontrollable bursts. Suddenly, something seems very funny and I have to laugh. Maybe it's because I've cried too much over the past few months. Either way, Sean looks incredulous, which just makes me giggle more.

"Nice, very nice, Avery. I like the suave way you avoided making me feel silly." Sean laughs with me after he says it. We both lean up against the car, giggling and gasping for air.

"Thanks," I finally say, looking over my shoulder at him. "I needed that."

"I'd take a door to the gut for you any time, Miss Smith." His eyes sweep over my face. They dart between my lips and my eyes. I think he's going to kiss me, but Sean takes a deep breath and pushes off the car. The moment is gone. "Come on. Let's get what we came here for."

Sean takes me by the hand and leads me into the toy store. We have to look on the clearance aisle because the thing he wants is out of season. He's bent over, digging around in a bin when he stands and grins at me.

"Found one." Sean plucks a kite from the bin, still wrapped in plastic. It has an extra-long thing of string.

"Are you serious? We came here for a kite?" I can't imagine what he's thinking.

"Yeah. My life could use a dash of levity right now." The way he says it, the way his voice catches in his throat, makes my heart ache. I feel the same way. He can see it in my eyes. "I suspect that you are in need of the same sort of, ah…screw it." Sean runs his fingers through his hair and looks at the floor before looking back up at me. "I'm trying to sound classy, Avery, but your eyes just make me melt. I can't think around you. You bring out a side of me that, well, let's just say that it hasn't seen sunlight in years. Let's go fly a kite at the beach. I'll buy you lunch. We can see how high the thing goes before the string snaps and it flies away. What do you say?"

Stepping toward him, I touch the plastic packaging on the little kite. It's the ninety-nine cent kind that kids fly. The corner of my lips pull up. "Well, I have plans this evening, but I think I can sneak in a trip to the beach to fly this…" Turning the package over, I look to see what cartoon character is on the kite. But when I flip it over, I laugh so hard that I slap my hands over my mouth. Giggling, I point to the kite. "Holy shit. That's a pig in a tutu! On a kite!"

Sean grins, "When pigs fly. Apparently, a very pretty pig will be flying today." He holds out his elbow. "My lady."

Laughing, I take his arm and embark on one of the best days of my life.

CHAPTER 6

I kick off my shoes as Sean pulls the little kite out of the package and assembles it. The beach is empty today, probably because it's freezing. The sun is a bright golden ball and the sky is an awesome shade of blue. I sit down and bury my toes in the sand, not caring about the chilly air.

Sean drops his coat on the sand next to me and ties the string onto the kite. "Here you go. Ladies first." Sean hands me the kite and I take it. I can't help but smile when I look at the thing. It has a pink cartoon pig doing a pirouette in a purple tutu. It's perfect.

"Just so you know, I suck at kite flying. Kites hate me. You've been warned." I nod at him, but Sean gives me a quizzical look.

"How could you possibly suck at kite flying?"

"Wait and see. It's the kind of suckage that's spectacular."

"Oh," he grins, saying, "the best kind of suckage, then." Sean takes the kite from my hands and walks a few steps back, after kicking off his shoes. The wind blows his dark hair out of his eyes. For the first time I get to see his face without that brooding look he always wears. Sean has a boyish grin on his face as he moves away from me holding the silliest kite that I've ever seen. "Ready?" he asks, and holds the kite over his head.

I nod. "Yup."

Sean releases the kite and I turn and run forward. The wind catches the kite quickly, pulling it higher and higher. I yank the line and let out more string and stop running. Then, I yank it again as the piggy kite swerves in the air. The wind pulls it hard and the kite changes direction. Sean is still standing in the same spot, looking up at the kite when it happens. I have no idea why it happens to me, but it does. The kite seems to get caught in a little vortex, swirls, and plummets—and I mean drops like a speeding vulture—from the sky. Sean's eyes grow wide. He runs at the last second and the kite crashes into his hip. He yelps and rubs his thigh.

I try not to laugh, but I can't hide the smile on my face. "I told you that I'm cursed. I can't fly a kite worth a damn. It doesn't matter where you stand. It *will* hit you." The wind catches my hair and tosses it behind me.

"I don't believe it," Sean says shaking his head as he walks toward me. "There is no way in hell you could hit me like that twice." Sean is standing next to me, winding up the string. He hands me the roll back and takes the kite. "Ready?"

"Hell, yeah. I'm fine. The kite isn't going to hit me. Maybe you should put on your helmet?" I tease him, grinning. I know how this is going to go. Sean's blue eyes lock with mine. A shiver runs through me and it has nothing to do with the crisp air.

"If you hit me again, I'll wear my helmet."

"Is that a challenge, Mr. Jones?"

"Are you doing it on purpose, Miss Smith? Were you a professional kite flyer or something?"

I laugh and shake my head. "No, it's just my natural awesomeness manifesting itself." I smile at him for a moment. "You know it's going to crash into you, right? I mean, this seems like we're tempting fate way too much."

"Fly the kite, Smitty." Sean steps away from me, spooling the string out as he walks. When he's a few feet away, Sean asks me if I'm ready.

I nod and he releases the kite. I tug the string hard and run a few steps. Sean moves this time and walks toward me. He watches the kite climb higher and higher.

I yank the string and the give it more slack. The piggy kite flies higher. Sean has that arrogant grin on his face, like he thinks he's won. He stands in the sand next to me and folds his arms over his chest. He's wearing jeans with a charcoal colored sweater. That color makes his eyes look like topaz.

Sean makes a pleased noise in the back of his throat. "The kite's still in the air."

"I didn't say that I couldn't keep it up," I grin at him. "That would be a totally different problem. I said that it will crash into you. To crash, the kite needs to come down. And it will hit you."

"That was a fluke. You can't honestly tell me that you've flown a kite in the past few years and it crashed into someone every time?"

"I could say no, but it'd be a big fat lie. Have a seat Mr. Jones and wait for it to happen." I tug the kite string and watch the piggy in the tutu dance against the sky.

Sean settles onto the sand next to me. He pulls up his knees and wraps his arms around them. "I used to come here a lot. It didn't matter what the weather was like."

I nod and glance at him out of the corner of my eye. "The best time to be here is—"

"Right before a storm," we say in unison.

Sean gives me a strange look, which I return. Smirking I tug on my piggy kite. A prickly feeling covers my skin and is gone in a flash. I tuck my hair behind my ear, but the wind keeps whipping it in my face. "Well, that was creepy. Most people say in the sunshine."

"You aren't most people."

"Neither are you," I say. My heart is pounding. I don't turn to look at him. I can feel his gaze resting on the side of my face. I tug the kite. "I like how the air feels thick and the waves crash onto the sand. I like to put my toes in the sand when it has that damp chill. I've come out in the rain, and just sat on the shore. There's something about the ocean, about the waves and watching a spring storm roll in that's soothing."

Sean stares at me. When he doesn't respond, I look over at him. His blue eyes are wide. When our gazes meet, they lock. I can't look away. Something inside me responds to him, to the way he looks at me. I feel the tug at the core of my body telling me that he's more than he seems. I try to force the sensation back, but I can't.

For a moment, Sean just breathes. When his lips part to say something, I feel the kite string go slack. Before the words are out of his mouth, the kite collides with his head. It falls to the sand in a pile of plastic and string. Sean jumps a mile, and holds his hand to his ear.

I step toward him, my feet getting tangled in string. "Are you all right?" I kneel in front of him and turn his face to the side.

Sean's hands fall away from the spot where he was hit. There's a little scrape on his cheek that's beading with blood. I reach into my pocket and take out a tissue. I press it to his skin and hold it there. I feel stupid for hurting him. Sean takes my hand in his. When I feel his gaze, I turn and look into his eyes. The wind ruffles his hair, tossing it every which way. He looks at me like he's never seen me before. The expression worries me. My stomach flips in response.

I manage, "I'm sorry."

Sean doesn't answer. He just watches me, intently focused on my face. Sean's eyes drift to my mouth. After a moment, he leans in and kisses me lightly. My lashes lower as he does it and my heart pounds harder. Sean pulls back slightly, and looks into my eyes. He opens his mouth like he's going to say something, but nothing comes out.

My voice is so sweet, so soft. I cup his face between my hands and say, "Oh, no. Did that blow to the head break your brain?"

Sean seems to come back from wherever his mind drifted off to. The panic in his eyes vanishes. I have back the flirt with the bike, the man with the kite. "If I'm bludgeoned by a piggy kite and lose my mind, you have to promise to tell people that I was done in by something much more manly."

I nod slowly, smiling. "Mmm. Bear attack. There are bears all over the beach. Totally believable." I wink at him.

"That mouth is going to get you in trouble," Sean says, smiling. The look in his eye is playful and carefree.

The kite is behind him. I lean forward, like I'm going to hug him. Sean tenses slightly. I have no idea why. We've had sex, how is he still tense when I touch him? The hug was a diversion anyway. I reach behind him and grab the kite.

Smacking the kite into his back, I giggle, saying, "Bear attack! Bear attack! Rwoar!"

Sean's jaw drops open. He lets me smack him with the kite at least three times before he tackles me, and knocks me back into the sand. Sean's fingers find my bare skin under my sweater and he tickles. I laugh and continue to taunt him. "Next time we should get a bear kite. That way it's more believable. Millionaire, Sean Ferro, attacked on Jones Beach, by a bear. Channel 12 will come running out if we call that in." I reach into my pocket, or rather I try to, but Sean yanks the phone away.

"I'm not a millionaire and Channel 12 doesn't cover bear attacks—too exciting." He pins me down, and manages to straddle me. Sean's breathing hard. He looks down at my face and I go still.

"You're not rich?"

"I didn't say that. I said I'm not a millionaire." Sean has a strange look on his face.

"Ah, since we're playing coy, I'm not a millionaire, either. I'm a twentyaire. I have twenty-five bucks in my pocket until I get paid." I try to pull my wrists free, but Sean doesn't budge. "So, come on. What are you? I told you how much I'm worth." I smile at him, laughing. "By the way, I'm paying for lunch. The $1 menu at Wendy's has some bitchin' chicken nuggets with your name on them." I waggle my eyebrows at him, not expecting him to tell me anything.

"You're treating me?" he asks, surprised. I nod. Sean pauses for a second. Then he licks his lips and leans down and whispers in my ear. "I'm a billionaire, maybe a few times over."

I giggle when he pulls back and say, "Like the Monopoly man?" I stare at him. Holy shit. Sean watches me, waiting to see how I take it. I act like I'm going to be serious, and ask, "Do you have that kickass top hat? Nah, I bet you're more of a monocle man." I reach into his pocket and Sean squirms.

He grabs my wrists and pins me again. "Seriously? That's your reaction? You ask me if I dress like a cartoon character?" My eyes shift back and forth between his. Sean seems surprised.

I'm more distracted by his eyes. I shrug. "Money's money. You need it to live, but beyond that, I don't care. You can't take it with you. Hey, and this doesn't mean that I'm going to stiff you on lunch. Don't worry. I'll get you a drink and some fries, too. What's mine is yours." I grin at him, expecting him to laugh, but he doesn't. The pressure on my wrists disappears as Sean sits up. He slips off of me and I sit up next to him. "Did I say something wrong?" I ask, tucking my hair behind my ear. "Because I do that a lot. I didn't mean to be ass-y Avery."

Sean glances at me. "You seriously only have twenty bucks?" I nod. "And you were going to spend most of it on me, today?"

I nod again. The way he's acting makes me nervous. I try to play it off, like it's nothing. "It's not rocket science, Sean. We're hungry. We eat."

Sean's eyes scan my face, like he can't believe what he sees. "You really don't have any desire to be rich?"

"There's a line between being piss-ass poor and having enough to get by. I want to hit the get-by line, maybe a little bit more." I shrug and pull my knees into my chest. "More than that just fucks things up. Life isn't about money. It's about the people you love—the relationships you make. Maybe I have that once poor always poor thing. I don't know, but I don't really care, Mr. Jones. If you have a problem with it—"

Sean stares at me like I have two heads. "I don't have a problem with it, not at all."

I wiggle my toes in the sand and say, "Can't buy me love."

To my surprise, Sean says the next line of the song. I smile at him. Sean continues to recite the verse and soon his words turn to song. The velvety sound of his voice sounds perfect. Sean pulls me to his chest and sings just for me. I relax, looking out at the ocean and watch the waves. His fingers smooth my hair as his breath warms my cheek. It makes that feeling in my chest stir, the good one. For the longest time, the only thing I could feel was that hollow ache.

CHAPTER 7

Sean nuzzles his chin to the side of my face and holds me tight. I'm sitting between his legs on the sand. The way he breathes makes me feel peaceful. It's strange. I don't understand why or how. I don't question things like that anymore. I just take it for what it is—I feel at ease around him. Sean rubs his hands over my arms. The chill in the air numbed my skin a while ago. It feels good to have him sitting so close, to warm me up.

I tilt my head back to ask him something, but never get the chance. When our eyes meet, something shifts. All day Sean has acted more like a friend than a lover. I've convinced myself it's because that's what he is. I'm his paid lover. It's not the same. But that look in his eye ensnares me. It pulls me to him, making the butterflies in my stomach flutter to life.

Sean watches my lips with a hungry intensity that sends sparks through my body. Through lowered lashes, his eyes never stray from my mouth. I'm pulled to him. With everything in me, I try to resist, but I can't. I'm barely breathing, hardly holding on. Sean gives me something to hold on to, at least for now.

The space between us closes. Sean's lips are right there. I feel the magnetic pull and before I know it, his lips are brushing against mine. I suck in air, trying hard to control myself. I don't want him to know how enamored I am, how much I want him. It has nothing to do with contracts or money. It's Sean. I want him, I want to be around him and taste his lips because I want to.

The kiss is a breathtaking tease. When he pulls away, Sean's blue eyes are blazing like twin flames. I can't look away. I twist in his lap and turn to my side. Leaning into his chest, I lift my hand to his cheek. Leaning in slowly, watching his beautiful lips, I close the space between us. My heart pounds harder as I feel Sean's hands in my hair. He doesn't pull me forward, but he doesn't push me back.

Something inside of me is screaming for me to stop. It's the voice that tells me to hold on, that I can survive this. When every other thought falls silent, it's always there. I don't understand the warning bells going off. I just know how Sean makes me feel and I need to feel something that I understand right now. That night on the motorcycle, the night he helped me chase my car down, there were no voices telling me to beware. He could have ridden off with me and dumped my body at the Captree boat docks. No one would have known what happened to me. There was no little voice in the back of my head then, so it's totally weird that it's there now.

Breathing in deeply, I ignore the warning and press my lips to his. The uncertainty fades as Sean kisses me back. His tongue sweeps against the seam of my lips, gently, asking me if I want him. When I let him in, Sean holds me tight and leans us back into the sand. He rolls so that I'm under him. The cold air and the hot kisses crash together. My pulse pounds harder as the kiss builds hotter and hotter. Sean keeps his lips on mine the entire time, not stopping for breath. His hands touch my face, gently stroking my cheek as the kiss intensifies. My heart thuds inside of me like it's been sleeping and suddenly startled awake. My body is hot and cold, my mind is swimming in sensations that conflict.

Sean knows how to draw me out of my despair. His touch is like magic. Everything that was crushing me is gone, temporarily held away. I lose myself in his lips. My eyes are closed and I focus on the feel of his lips on mine. Every time he sweeps his tongue over mine, my insides flutter. It's magic.

After a moment, Sean pulls back. His eyes sweep my face before locking with mine. Reaching toward me, Sean tucks a dark curl behind my ear. "Your kiss is addicting," he says, his voice a little too husky from a kiss. I smile at him and touch his cheek and feel the light stubble under the pads of my fingers. Sean's eyes lower as I do it. He takes a slow, deep, breath like he's savoring my touch. When his eyes open again, he takes a jagged breath. My gaze drifts to his lips. I can't stop staring at his mouth. "If you keep looking at me like that, I'm not going to be able to stop."

An awkward smile spreads across my face. My fingers twirl the hair at the base of his neck. "You'd have sex in the sand, when it's freezing outside?"

"If it meant that I could be with you," his hand strokes my cheek, "then, yes."

I stare into Sean's eyes, unable to blink, unable to breathe. This feels real. I don't know what to say. "You get to be with me as much as you want. You bought me, remember?"

Sean's eyes dart back and forth between mine. His hand strokes my cheek again. The sensation makes my eyes close briefly as his warm fingers trail across my chilled skin. "But it's not like this."

Before I can ask him what he means,
Sean's lips are on mine. He kisses me
fiercely, pressing his mouth firmly to mine.
His hands rove my body, carefully moving
over areas that no one is supposed to touch.
His hands slip over the curve of my hips
and under my sweater. I feel Sean's cold
fingers press against the small of my back. I
arch toward him and Sean pulls me tighter.
He kisses me like he's never going to get
another chance.

My fingers tangle in his hair. I find the
bottom of his sweater and slip my hands
underneath. I slide my palms along his
toned body, feeling the warm skin on his
back. Sean reacts by moving onto me. My
knees part and I wrap my ankles around his.
The kisses grow more passionate. My heart
pounds harder. I don't understand how he
does this to me. In that moment, there's
only him and me. I don't hurt. There are no
memories to repress, no thoughts to hold
back. There's only Sean and his hot lips.

Without realizing it, I pull his hair. Sean
gasps and breaks the kiss. His eyes are dark
with desire. He's breathing hard and so am
I. Watching me closely, Sean reaches for the

button on my jeans. He flips the button with his thumb and lowers the zipper. My pulse is thundering in my ears, waiting to see what Sean wants to do. His blue eyes are locked on mine. Sean presses his hand to my stomach and slips his fingers into my panties. My mouth falls open into a little O. I make a sound at the back of my throat as his fingers touch me. Sean watches me and gages my reactions to his touch. He moves his hand in a way that makes me hot even though it's cold.

Sean's fingers tease me, pressing and flicking the sensitive flesh. I gasp and push my hips to his hand, wanting more. He watches me move. Our eyes lock. There's something about his gaze that captivates me. I never thought I'd want someone to do this to me, and watch me so openly, but with him it feels right. When I can't stand the teasing anymore, I wrap my fingers around Sean's neck and pull him back down. Kissing Sean fiercely, I feel his hand shift lower. His fingers push inside of me. Gasping, I rock my hips against his hand. Sean dips his fingers in and out, rocking with me. The movement makes me feel like

I'm floating. I never want it to end. I feel his eyes on me, watching me. My heart pounds harder. I feel what he's done to me, how my body responds to him. The heat between my legs warms my entire body.

Sean's lips press against my cheek and then dip to my neck. I hear voices coming from somewhere behind us on the boardwalk. Sean hears them, too. He stills for a moment and the people walk past. Sean is breathing hard when he looks at me.

"Tell me what you want," Sean says, his voice filled with need.

"You." It's the only thing I want. I want to feel Sean inside of me. I want to lose myself in him.

I reach for his jeans and undo the button. When my hands are on the zipper, he stops me. Sean's fingers hold mine. There's a slight tremor to his hands. When I look at his face, Sean won't return my gaze. I can barely breathe. Sean seems like he's frozen. I must have done something, but I don't know what. Taking his hand, I lift it to my lips. I kiss each one of his fingers, gently pressing my lips to the soft pad. Then, I take the next finger and do it again. When I finish, I reach for his waist again.

This time, Sean lets me. I lower his zipper and slip my hand below his jeans. Sean sucks in the cold air as my fingers wrap around his hard, hot shaft. I free him from his cloths without undressing him, and then pull him onto me. Sean adjusts my jeans, lowering them. When the cold air hits my warm bottom, I think I might die. But then Sean is there, hot and hard.

I feel his body against mine. Sean pushes into me slowly and then pulls nearly all the way out. Then he repeats it. My hands find the skin on his back. Every time he pushes into me, I dig my nails in wanting more. Every moment that passes is filled with pure bliss. My body responds to him, but it's so different than the other night. I feel different. My core is hotter than hell and that delicate throbbing starts somewhere inside of me. Sean thrusts into me in rhythm with that pulsing. As he takes me higher and higher, the throbbing becomes more demanding. When he can't take it anymore, Sean thrusts into me, pushing harder and faster, until I shatter.

Gasping, every inch of my body feels incredible. I'm so high, so intoxicated with him.

Sean stays there, on top of me, breathing hard. His fingers brush my hair out of my face. The look on his face is pensive. Sean's gaze sweeps over my eyes, cheeks, and lips. His mouth parts like he wants to say something, but he doesn't. A shiver slips down my spine. Suddenly I feel the cold sand and damp air. I'm still warm, but my senses are returning. I'm falling back to earth, becoming more aware of what we did.

Sean rolls off of me and helps me get my jeans up without filling them with sand. As it is, there's sand stuck to my cheeks and the small of my back. We wiggled too much to be sand-free. After he buttons my jeans, Sean lays back down, pressing his body to mine. That distant look in his eyes is gone, replaced with something that I don't recognize. There's a softness there, a vulnerability that makes me want to hold him forever. Sean presses his lips together. I think he's going to say something, but he can't seem to say it. I start to speak, but

Sean leans down and presses his lips to mine, silencing me. The kiss is small and chaste. His mouth drifts to my cheek, and then my eyes and nose, leaving a trail of light kisses in his wake. The last kiss is on my forehead.

I watch him, wondering what he's thinking, wishing that I knew. I finally ask, "What are you thinking?"

Sean sits up on the sand and lets out a rush of air. He pushes his hands through his hair and looks down at me. "I wish things were different. I wish I..." He sounds tense, like he made a mistake. The muscle in his jaw tightens like he can't swallow.

I sit up and lean back on my elbows. The wind catches my hair and lifts it from my neck, chilling me. I jump up. I reach out and take Sean's hand and pull him to his feet. "This isn't the time for wishing or regrets."

Sean looks at my hands holding onto his. When his gaze lifts, he asks, "Then what time is it?" There's more there, things he wants to say. I can hear his heart breaking all over again. I wonder if I'm echoing his wife. I wonder if he feels guilty. I know loss, but Sean's is different. I can't imagine his pain.

"Time for lunch. I'm treating. You're driving. Come on, motorcycle man. Carpe diem and all that crap. Let's go!" I bend over and grab the piggy kite and we head for the car.

Neither of us says anything for a while. Sean seems lost, like he's floating with no anchor. I lean back in the seat, grateful for the heater. Maybe I'm a little nuts, always making myself cold, but that doesn't mean that I don't like getting warm. I like things that are predictable, things that I can control. It makes me feel better.

We head into Wendy's and I tell Sean to grab us a table. He lifts an eyebrow at me. "You're ordering for me? That's kind of manly."

"Get over it, bitch," I tease, smiling at him. I meant it to sound more serious, but he smiles and I laugh. "Go sit. Let me treat you to the most wonderful lunch of your life." I lean in and whisper in his ear, "It's *that* good."

Sean walks away and I order us a bunch of stuff off the cheap-o menu. This is a splurge for me, but it's worth it. I get the idea that Sean doesn't dine on a $1.99 very often. I wonder what expression he'd have on his face if saw my dorm room and my stash of Ramen noodles. The naked guy would probably be a distraction. Where the hell did he get a turkey from, anyway? I wonder if Amber's plaything stole it from the cafeteria.

I smile to myself and walk back to the table. Sean looks at the tray and back up at me. "Milkshakes?"

"Don't come between a girl and her chocolate. Here," I hand him a small burger, half the fries, and a cup of chili. Taking the burger, I unwrap it and pull the bun off. I spoon the chili onto the meat, followed by the fries, and then a dollop of the shake. "Happy lunch."

Sean looks at the sandwich like it might bite him. He tilts his head sideways and looks at the frozen shake melting out the side of the sandwich. "And you can assure me that I won't die from eating this?" He lifts it and takes a bite. There's a crazy-ass expression on his face, like he can't decide if it's delicious or disgusting.

I shrug my shoulders as I make my own weird little burger. "I don't know. This is the first time I've put these together." When I put the bun back on and lift the burger to my mouth, Sean's blue eyes are wide. He's staring at me. "What?"

"I'm waiting to see if you're screwing with me or if you plan on eating it, too." He's smiling, like he's trying not to laugh.

"Oh, I'm eating it." I grin at him and stuff the food in my mouth, taking a huge bite. The lettuce and ice cream are cold, while the rest of it is hot. The textures and tastes mix in mouth.

Sean watches me chew. "What's your verdict?"

I smile and wipe some chocolate from the corner of my mouth. "It's the most confusing thing I've ever eaten. It's sweet and salty, hot and cold. It's like the bipolar burger."

"Created by the slightly insane spray-start car girl," Sean says smiling at me. He takes another bite and makes a strange face when he swallows. I can't believe he's eating it. "I still can't decide if it's good or gross."

I point a fry at him and say, "Eat the whole thing and then decide."

"I think you're just trying to see what you can put in my mouth, Miss Smith." Sean's eyes sparkle as he leans across the table and speaks in that velvety voice of his.

I poke him in the nose with a French fry. "I already know what I can put in your dirty mouth, Mr. Jones."

He feigns shock and presses his fingers to his chest. "And I've barely told you about myself. My, my, what keen eyes you have...amongst other things." There's an older guy at the next table. He glances at Sean, his eyes wide.

My face flames red. I hide behind my burger, acting like I'm going to take a bite, but it just hovers in front of my face. Sean presses a finger to the food and pushes it back to the table. I glance up at Sean. There's a wicked look in his eye. "How can you be so shy after what we just did? There were people, Avery, and you didn't even pause. But this, talking about it later, this makes you blush?" He's laughing, smiling at me, teasing.

I slap his arm. "I'm a complicated person, what can I say?"

The man next to us clears his throat. He's thin, with leathery looking skin and silver hair. A green ball cap sits on his head. He's wearing a flannel jacket. With his tray in his hand, he stands and says to me, "Be careful with that one." His eyes flick to Sean as he passes us, like the old guy doesn't like him.

The smile fades off of Sean's lips, but I call after the guy. "Actually it's the other way around."

The old guy gives me a look when he dumps the trash off his tray. He walks out without another word.

"So, random men warn you away from me and that's your response?" Sean looks at me oddly. I can't tell if he's playing with me or really wants to know.

"Random men say lots of things to me. One guy was like, *that guy stole your car!* He was really sexy. Turns out that he's a bit of a sex fiend." I laugh lightly and smile at him. Sean's eyes hold mine and I feel my stomach sink. I said the wrong thing.

But Sean glazes over it. "I was kind of shocked. Most girls would scream and call the cops if they got carjacked."

I point a fry at him and say, "I'm not most girls. I flashed half of Long Island that night jumping on and off your bike."

Sean watches me. I can tell he's going to say something terrible. I don't want to hear it. I try to talk over him, but he puts his hand over mine and cuts me off. "You know that things can't stay like this, don't you? I'm not this guy."

I don't understand what he means. How can he not be himself? But, suddenly his words snap into place. There's a darker version of Sean. This lighter one isn't real. It's an illusion. I pull my hand away and pick at my food. "That's fine. I'm not this girl."

"Avery," he snaps, with a *be serious* tone.

"Sean," I mimic him back, using the same voice. "Don't tell me what I do or don't see. I know you're a fucked up mess, okay. So am I. I'm okay with it."

"You don't know what you're talking about." His voice is cold, warning. The rest of the meal passes in tense silence. I don't know what to say to him. After everything that happened today, I feel closer to him and this feels like he's pushing me away. I don't understand why. Every time things seem okay, he acts like this. It's driving me crazy.

Sean's gaze doesn't meet mine while he finishes eating. It's like he's stuck somewhere in the back of his mind. I wonder if he can't come out of that darkness or if he doesn't want to. The entire time I'm with him, I notice something. We're very alike in how we dealt with the lot we were given, but there's a cynical sharpness to Sean that I don't have. He seems to guard it, carefully wielding it when someone gets too close. That smile on his face, the one he wore that night at the steakhouse, is fake. His entire façade is a house of cards. I can't blame him for doing anything he needs to do to hold himself together. I don't pretend to know how he feels about his loss. It's almost like he blames himself, that it was more than misfortune that stole his wife. I glance at his beautiful face and wonder about his child. I can't imagine Sean giving the baby away, not if that child is the last piece he has of his wife. But Sean doesn't mention the baby.

My throat tightens thinking about it. Sean's lived through hell and hides every last bit of it. Watching him at the cemetery was the first glimpse I got of who he really is, and every time that I think I know Sean, I find out that I don't know him at all.

After lunch, Sean drives me back to campus. The silence continues, until he turns onto the main road. "Do I need to pretend that I don't know where you live? Or would you like me to drop you by your dorm?"

I glance at him. How does he know which dorm I'm in? I wonder if I should be concerned, but I'm not. Not looking at him, I say, "Wherever is fine." My emotions feel brittle like an old leaf. I'm afraid I'm going to lose myself and never crawl out of the grief that's drowning me.

Sean pulls up in front of my dorm. I get out and see my car parked at the end of the lot. Before I shut the door, I turn back. "Thank you." My voice is wrong. It sounds like I'm saying something else, something I should never say to him. *I love you.* I hold his gaze for a moment and try to swallow, but I can't.

Sean nods. "Thank you. I'll remember today for a very long time."

My throat tightens. Why does it feel like we're saying good-bye? I push back the feelings, and nod at him. I close the door and walk away, thinking I'll see him in a few hours. But, I'm wrong.

CHAPTER 8

As I walk toward my room, I pass Mel, who darts from her room when she sees me walk by. I don't feel like talking and I need to change.

Mel doesn't seem to care though, and yanks me by the elbow. "Whoa! Where do you think you're going?" I whirl around and catch my balance before I fall over. Sand falls out of my pant leg onto the dingy gray carpet. Mel glances at the sand and back up at me. She crosses her arms over her ample chest and throws out her hip. Her head sways as she scolds me. "Have you lost your mind? I saw you with that guy on the beach. You can't date anyone. Get your ass in here." When I don't move and flick my eyes longingly down the hallway, she snaps her fingers. "Now."

I sigh. "Fine. Whatever." I follow her into her room. Her roommate is out. Mel has at least nine books open with pages marked with little sticky notes. She's working on her research project.

"Don't give me that shit, Avery. I saw you and if I saw you, Black could have." She shuts the door. After moving a book, she extends her hand to the chair I usually take when I visit her room. "Sit, and tell me what the hell you're thinking. Black won't pay you a cent if you violate your contract, which— by the way—you did by making out with some guy on the beach."

My eyes feel tired, strained. I glance up at her. "How'd you find me?"

She cocks her head to the side and makes a face. "Do you think I'm stupid?" Tapping her finger to her lips, she says, "Let's see, what are the three places Avery runs off to when she's psychotically upset?"

Mel ticks them off on her finger as she lists my three places. "One, that shitty old church out in timbuckfuckingtoo, which is a hell of a drive to make when you're not already out there. Two, your parent's grave. And three, Jones Beach, Field five. Seriously, what the hell is going through your head?" She folds her arms over her chest and taps her foot. Mel is still standing in front of me. I know she's scolding me because she knows what's at stake—everything, my whole life.

I don't look at her when I speak. "I didn't realize you knew all those places."

"A girl can't have a brain? Since your parents died, I know exactly where to find you when you go into that super funk, but Avery—after everything you went through to get that job and you already did the nasty with a client—why are you throwing it away?" Her arms fall to her sides and her voice softens a little.

"I'm not," I say, feeling emotionally barren. "The guy on the beach was Sean. I ran out to the cemetery. You're right about that." She nods like *damn straight I'm right.* I glance up at her. "Please sit. Today's been hard and I really don't need you towering over me like you're going to strangle me."

Mel grumbles and then plops down on her bed. "Go on."

"Sean was there. I didn't see him at first." I feel the story stick in my throat. I don't want to talk about it, but I need to. I tell her about the paper that fell out of his coat, his wife's name, about what I thought. "But I was wrong. She died and I don't know what happened to the baby, he doesn't talk about it. He's hollow, like me." I'm staring into nothing as I speak. My voice echoes in my ears. I feel like I'm not even here anymore.

"Bullshit." Mel rushes toward me, which shocks the hell out of me. Grabbing me by the shoulders, she pins me back in the chair. She shakes me hard, yelling in my face as she does it. "Wake the fuck up!" Mel releases me. I blink rapidly and look at her like she's nuts. "You think this is a game? You don't have the luxury to have that spaced out look on your face. One mistake Avery, just one goddamned mistake will send you into cardboard-box-land and you'll never come back.

"This was a mistake. You're falling for him. That's a bigger mistake. There's nothing there for you. The guy is fucked up beyond repair. He hired a call girl so he wouldn't have to deal with whatever shit happened to him. It's none of your business. He's not yours. He never will be, so stop thinking about him like that.

"This will ruin you, Avery. Maybe you don't see it yet, but I sure as hell do. And you're not like him. I know you think you are, I see it on your pasty face, but you're not. He has no soul. That guy is dead inside. You aren't. You're still fighting. Don't give up, girl. As your best friend, as a girl who's had her share of shit, don't surrender. You and me, we're survivors. You're going to get through this. You're going to finish college, get your master's degree, and get the hell out of here. I know you will."

Mel's passion is contagious. I feel incredibly stupid for moping around, for attaching myself to someone who doesn't want me. Swallowing hard, I ask, "How do you know? I mean, Sean seems—"

Mel leans toward me and places her hand on my shoulder. "Listen. I'm going to tell you how I know, and don't think that I'm mean. I'm just telling you what's real, okay?" I nod slowly. Fear pulses through my body. I can already tell that I'm not going to like what she has to say. "That guyy doesn't love you. He's not even into you. He came to Black and asked for a virgin. That was it, Avery. You were the only one, so he took you. I was there when he called. He wanted a curvy blonde. Black said all we had was you. You're not his type. You're a warm pussy to fuck and nothing more. Avery, do your job and get the hell away from him." She tightens her grip on my shoulder.

I can't look at her. Inside my head, I know that's all I am. I'm a hooker, but sometimes it feels like more. My jaw locks as she speaks. When I try to talk, I work it to loosen the tense muscles. "You're right. I know you're right..."

"And?"

"And, nothing. I'm nothing to him. All this is new to me. I can't separate my heart from my body." I blink slowly, trying to get the burning sensation in my eyes to stop.

Mel sits down across from me, but still within reach. "Admitting that it's just sex is the first part. Doing it over and over again is what steels your heart. When you do it that way, you don't know who they are and you won't care. It's money, it's a stress-reliever, it's fun—but it's never love. Avery, you've got to remember that. They want no strings, no emotional attachment, and that's what we give them." Mel pauses for a second and then glances at me, like she shouldn't be asking. "What do you think about taking another client? It would help you get over this one."

"I already told Black that I would." My chest feels like it's going to cave in. The pressure's too much.

"Good. Good." Mel pats my knee. "That's the first step out of this. When you do it with another guy, you'll see that what you feel for Sean is just a trick your mind's playing on you; that it was only fucking. If you told Black that you want another client, she'll have you agree to the person and sign the contract tonight before going to Sean. Sign them. Don't wait. It'll keep things from getting more muddled. You can do this, Avery. It's a good job." Her eyes are so vibrant. She's leaning toward me, trying to hold my gaze.

I nod slowly, like I'm stuck in a vat of gelatin. "I know it is, but I don't know if I can shut him out. How do I do that?" I ask, glancing up at her. I feel so lost, so alone. I bury my face in my hands and breathe.

"It's a job, Avery. Keep things that way. Let him lead and don't kiss him, don't give the chance for anything else. The guy has got to have some fetish shit going on. Drag it out of him and do it. That'll shatter your prince charming version of him real fast." She pats my knee again, and then grabs my hands and pulls me up. "You need some fun." I start to protest, but she waves me off. "No, I know you gotta get ready, but you'll like this fun. Come on."

Mel drags me down the hallway and stops in front of my door. She grins at me with mischief her eyes. Mel presses her fingers to her lips, telling me to be quiet. Then she turns the knob and kicks open the door. The door makes a loud thud. Naked guy is standing at the counter. He jumps a mile. I can't believe he's still here. I look around for Amber. The light in the bathroom is on and the shower is running.

Mel walks in, sashaying her hips and making a beeline for naked dude. I follow her in and watch, leaving the door open behind me.

"Hey, ladies," he grins at us, "Is it time for a threesome? I got my—" The smile falls off his face. Concern flashes in his eyes when he sees Mel coming for him.

"I want you to take your skinny ass out of this room and never come back." As she walks, Mel passes the turkey carcass and takes the carving knife. Mel flips it in her hand like she's a ninja. My mouth falls open. So does naked guy's.

He lifts his palms, "Ladies, please. I can do you both separately. That's not a problem." His normal bravado is gone. His voice sounds like it's stuck in his throat. Mel flips the knife. It turns handle over blade several times and then she catches it in her hand.

"Sure, pasty. Let's do it. I've got a bit of a pain fetish though, so let's just say that this won't be pleasant—for you." Mel smiles at him.

Naked guy doesn't speak. He glances across the room. His clothes are at the foot of Amber's bed. He smiles at Mel like he's going to say yes, then turns on his heel and runs. Naked guy nearly knocks me over, muttering *crazy bitches* under his breath and tears down the hallway. Laughter follows in his wake. Mel grins at me, and stabs the knife into the cutting board.

A few seconds later, we see naked guy running across the quad, out the window. I laugh. Apparently his exhibitionism was only for a lucky few ladies, because he's screaming like a lunatic as he runs for the bookstore. I wonder if he plans on buying new clothes or hiding in the stacks.

"You knife juggling nut," I say to Mel, laughing.

"Nobody plays wussy games like darts, not where I'm from." She laughs and looks out the window. "Did you see his face?"

I did. Smiling, I joke, "I think Amber lost her fuck-buddy."

As if summonsed, Amber appears in the bathroom doorway. Her hair is wrapped in a towel and she's wearing a ratty old robe. She rolls her eyes when she sees us. "Get out of here, bitch," she says to Mel, which was a mistake. No one says that to Mel.

Mel walks over to her and growls in her face, "What'd you call me, you little piece of—"

I tug Amber's arm. She doesn't move. I hiss in her ear, "That was like the worst thing you could have called Mel. All those rumors about her growing up in the hood are true and you just pissed her off. You might want to run before she rips your face off."

Amber comes to life. She frantically mutters things that make no sense and finally says, "I have to go." She races out the door in her robe and doesn't come back.

I hug Mel and say, "I owe you one. Thank you."

She nods. "What are friends for if they can't chase off hoes and guys with little winkies?" We both laugh. Mel turns to leave and says, "Get dressed in peace. I'll check in with you in the morning. We can have pancakes. I'm running a syrup deficit."

I watch her walk away. Confidence lines her shoulders, even though her life has sucked. It's made her stronger and she's better for it. I'm done moping. I'm not letting my past consume me. I don't care what it takes. I'll survive because I want to—on my own terms. Fuck everything else. I deserve a happy life.

CHAPTER 9

After I'm all decked out for work, I feel strange. It's like part of me wants to turn cold so I can endure this fate. The other part of me whispers in the back of my mind, telling me that things can still be warm and safe. I need to smack her over the head with a frying pan. That little voice in the back of my head is going to ruin me. She never stops hoping, even when there's nothing left to hope for. I gag that fragment of my brain and lock her away with my pride. Tonight is about getting to tomorrow. It's about surviving and that's it. Nothing else matters.

My dress swishes against my bare thighs as I take the stairs two at a time. My Chucks are on my feet in case I have issues with my car. There are always issues with my car. If I really take more clients, like Mel encouraged me to do, I can replace the misfit car with something that actually runs. I'd like that. But maybe not. This car is one of the only connections I have to my father. I worked on it with him, taping it up when it dumped oil all over the drive way. It's always been a bad car, but maybe I'll keep it anyway.

As I round the corner, I run into Amber. She's sitting on the stairs with her face in her hands, all hunched over. I came this way to avoid people. As it is, I got three cat calls walking down the hallway and one was from a girl. I pause. There's nothing I'd like more than to kick Amber and run down the stairs laughing, but I don't.

I sigh dramatically and sit next to her, ignoring the dirty floor and my insanely expensive dress. "Hey, bitch," I say teasingly. "Why are you hiding in the stairwell?"

Amber lifts her face. It's covered in a sheen of tears and snot. Gross. I hand her a tissue. She takes it and looks at me like I'm insane. "Are you here to gloat?"

"No, I came this way so no one would see me spray-start my car. It's parked at the end of the building in that dark lot. As soon as I put the hood up, guys flock over like I'm too stupid to start my own car."

She snorts, "Yeah, well…" I can tell she has something nasty on her tongue, but Amber swallows it and looks sheepish. "You have more guts than me. I've put my hood up, if you know what I mean, just to get a guy to talk to me."

"Yeah, I realize that. You're a prickly bitch when you want to be, but it's like you're bipolar or something because there's a sassy smart mouth in there too. I'm guessing she lost that battle of the alter egos."

Amber holds onto her knees and dabs her face with the tissue. "Yeah, something like that. It's easier to get guys to like me when I act like that."

"You know they don't really know you, right? I mean, if that's not really you. At this point, I'm not really sure who you are."

"Me neither," Amber says. Turning her head toward me, she looks at me and finally sees me. "What are you wearing?"

I shrug, suddenly feeling nervous. "Nothing. I have a date and can't wear heels driving my car. It stalls a lot."

"I heard you chased down some dick who stole that car out from under you." There's an expression on her face that I haven't seen before—respect.

"I did. Several times." Wonderful, my legacy is being the crazy chick that chases a car that's well past its expiration date.

"I wish I had guts like that. It's like you don't care what people think of you." There's a far off look in her eye, like she can't fathom being that way.

I don't know how to answer her. My life is a mess. I stand and say, "The room's empty if you want it. I won't be back tonight." I start to walk down the stairs.

Amber calls after me. "Where's your crazy friend?"

"Out," I call back, and then I'm out of sight. I don't understand that girl. Awh, hell, I don't understand anything. I should really stop trying. I spend half my life trying to get a grip on things, but they just slip through my fingers in the end. I'm lucky I know my ass from my elbow. There's no clear cut answer for anything anymore.

The air is crisp and cold. My breath makes little white clouds the moment I walk outside. I tug my ratty sweater over my head, carefully not to mess up my hair. I think about the way I felt earlier today, the way Sean called me on torturing myself with the weather. Maybe I should stop doing that. I don't know. It's one of the few comforts I have. How fucked up is that? Freezing myself is comforting. Damn, I need a shrink.

I spray the can of ether and slam the hood shut. Jumping in, I start the car. It warbles to life sounding like a spastic birdsong. I rev the engine and back out. The car doesn't stall once on my way to Miss Black's. Tonight might not suck so much after all.

Holy hell, was I wrong.

CHAPTER 10

I strip and weigh in, again. It seems redundant since I was here last night, but since Sean let me leave for the middle of the day, Miss Black does everything again. I'm wearing the same dress as yesterday. I didn't have anything else.

Miss Black holds it out and shakes her head. "This is a major infraction." She takes the dress and tosses it onto her chair. It sits behind her desk getting wrinkled. I'm standing in front of her in my freshly laundered lingerie from the other night. She's not happy about that either.

"I haven't been paid, yet. I took this job because I'm broke. This is all I have."

"Yes, well. Be glad that we have some wardrobe for photo shoots." She plucks something from her closet. "Put this on." It's a tiny black piece of fabric that looks way too small to be a dress.

I eye it and do what she says. As I'm wiggling into the dress, Black takes a box from the bottom drawer of her desk and unlocks it. She removes cash and the book I saw the first night that I was here with Mel. I barely have the dress on when she says, "Leave it. It's supposed to sit high on the thigh, but this—" she tugs the neckline, straightening it. The dress is form fitting. I feel like a sausage shoved into a balloon. There's no way I look hot, but I don't comment. The black dress clings to me. There's a keyhole opening that reveals my cleavage. The skirt hugs my hips tightly and barely covers my panties.

"There, that's better. Now turn." I do as she says. Miss Black grabs my shoulders and I stop. I feel her gaze on my back. She thrusts her hand forward. "Give them to me. You can't wear that kind of panty with this dress. Panty lines are ungodly."

I freeze. I am not going commando in this tiny skirt. "I don't think—" I start to say, but she cuts me off.

Snapping her fingers, Miss Black huffs, "No one cares that you were prude, Avery. Hand over the panties so we can get on with things." Reluctantly, I shimmy them down and fork them over. I tug at the hem of the dress, but Miss Black slaps my hands away. "Leave it. Oh, and before I forget, here's an advance on your paycheck. Spend it wisely." She hands me several large bills. I reach for the money and stuff it in my purse.

Miss Black continues, "You can pick up your clothes tomorrow when you check in. One more thing before you leave. Here is your next client." She turns the big book toward me and points to a page. "I need you to update your preferences sheet and sign."

I glance at the papers. The man is a little older, but still attractive. He's not Sean. With every fiber of my being, I don't want to do this, but I have no choice. I lift the pen and sign the contract. There. Done. I start to walk away.

Miss Black stops me, "Avery, your preference sheet?" She pushes it toward me and sits down behind her desk. I look back at the paper.

"I don't care. Whatever he wants."

Black looks at me like I don't understand what I've said. "Avery, dear, I think you'll—"

"I don't care," I say more pointedly this time. "Whatever he wants. It's all the same to me."

Black smiles like she won the lottery. "I'm pleased to hear it. You'll fetch a higher price with that attitude."

I smile back at her like I'm excited, but I'm not. I leave the building and duck into the limo waiting at the curb. I slip back into my seat and slouch. I pick at my nails for a moment and then stop so that I won't ruin the polish.

How quickly things change. A few nights ago I was so nervous that I nearly puked. Now, I just want to go and get it over with. Staring out the window, I remind myself that this isn't real. It doesn't matter what Sean says or does, this isn't love.

CHAPTER 11

I hate how short my dress is, but I walk with confidence the way Miss Black told me to and step into the elevator. When I emerge, the hotel restaurant is in front of me. I pass the hostess at the podium and wave at her, like I'm here every day. Lately, I've been here too much. She nods and I walk into the restaurant, past poshly decorated tables to find Sean seated in the same location in the back. He has that look on his face, and the same dark intensity lurks behind his eyes as the first night.

Lifting his gaze, Sean runs his eyes over me, taking in every curve. His lips don't move. There's no expression on his face. I don't sit. Instead, I stand there, waiting for him to say something. Sean's cold again. This feels like a business transaction and nothing more. Now I understand why he does it. It's because he has to. There's no way to be both warm and contained at the same time.

Sean lifts his steely gaze. I step forward and press my finger to the monogram on his plate. His eyes lock with mine. My heart tries to race faster when he looks at me, but I forbid it. I can be cold, too. I shut everyone else out. What's one more person? I'm not sure why I let him into my messed up life in the first place.

Sean arches a brow at me, but my meaning is clear. Whatever happened this morning is gone. Things are back to the status quo now. Sean nods and extends his arm, waving me to sit. "Avery," he says my name like we're strangers.

My stomach feels like I ate a window—wood, glass, and all—and churns uncomfortably. The waiter appears from nowhere when I take my seat. He pulls back the chair for me and I sit down. Sean orders wine and the waiter disappears.

"Nice dress," he says, carelessly.

"Nice tie," I say, leaning to the side, like I don't care. Sean looks stunning. He's wearing a black suit with a black shirt. His silk tie is midnight blue which makes his eyes look bluer than I would have thought possible.

Sean smirks. "I wouldn't have thought you'd wear something like that." Sean is mirroring me. I pretend not to notice. I sit up and tilt my head, making my hair fall over my shoulder.

"Yeah, well, it turns out that I do." I lean closer to him and give him a lazy smile. "Before I left, Black stripped me and stole my panties, so half the work's done for you." I wink and sit back.

Sean is still leaning forward. His cool façade cracks a little. "You're not wearing panties under that?" I shake my head slowly and smile at him. It seems to do something to him, but he tries to hide it. Sean's voice sounds a little too breathy when he speaks. "Well then, it's only fair to tell you that…"

he leans closer. I lean in to hear him whisper, taking a sip of wine as he speaks. "I'm not wearing any panties either."

I try so hard not to react to him, but I can't help it. I snort laugh and choke on the wine. It's so embarrassing. I keep coughing and I can't stop. Sean smiles at first and then looks concerned. He moves his chair closer to me, leaning in and placing his hand on my back. "Are you okay?"

I punch his arm and he sits back and smiles. Everyone is looking at us. "You're such an ass," I hiss.

Sean scoots back to his place. The grin on his face lights him up. I can't picture him looking more perfect than he does right now. "You started it, Miss Smith. I suggest you only step up to the net if you intend to play hard."

"Tennis euphemisms? Really? Nothing says highbrow like tennis," I lift the glass and make snobby face. I suck at not letting him affect me. Within minutes of arriving, Sean cracked my shell and is pulling me out, but I can't have it.

"Well, the balls are the right size…" he opens his hands like he's explaining something that would be rational.

I laugh. I can't help it. "Not for you, they're not."

"Flattery will get you nowhere, Miss Smith."

"I already have a free pass into your panties after dinner, Mr. Jones. I expect my flattery to get me everywhere and then some." I sip my wine again with a smug look on my face.

Sean's expression shifts from neutral to that lazy sultry look that's so damn hot. "Where exactly is the *and then some*. It sounds titillating." He strokes his chin, drawing my eye to his lips as he does it.

"Check my preference sheet. It's recently been updated."

Sean's smirk falters, but he puts it back. The movement is so fast that I'm not sure I saw it. Maybe I just hope that I did. "Is that so?"

I nod and tap my finger nail once against my wine glass. "You can titillate anything you want. No restrictions. No hang ups."

Sean just stares at me. After a moment, he asks, "Why the change in pace?"

I avert my gaze and trace my finger around the curve of the glass. "Why not? I mean, that is if you're willing to. Unless, you're only into fake relationship kind of sex…" Sean stares at my lips like he wants to devour them. He doesn't speak.

"Oh, come on," I say, leaning closer to him. I take his tie between my fingers and feel the silky fabric with my thumb. Sean looks at my hand and slowly returns his gaze to my face. "You've got to have some fetish or kinky desire, something that you *need*." I say the last word slowly, wrapping my lips around the syllables.

Sean sits perfectly still, like he's under a spell. It breaks when the waiter comes back and puts our food down on the table. Sean lifts his fork. He doesn't talk about my offer. Instead, he points at me with a fork and says, "Eat."

Dinner progresses in silence. I don't like eating with him. It feels too informal, too personal. He knows what food I like. The meal on my plate wasn't listed on the menu. It's a salty sweet lover's paradise with sweet sundried cranberries, sprinkles of feta cheese, and pork so savory that it melts in my mouth. There's some kind of sweet glaze over the meat. I could die. It's perfectly delicious. I chew slowly, wishing that Sean's thoughtfulness didn't appeal to me, but it does.

After dinner, Sean stands and takes my hand, pulling me up. With my heels on, I can look directly into his eyes. They captivate me and swallow me whole. The floor of my stomach falls away. I suck at this. I don't know how I'm supposed to do this and not be affected by him. Sean tells the waiter to send up the desserts in an hour or so. He takes my hand and leads me to the elevators.

Someone tries to come in with us, but Sean says, "Sorry, better catch the next one." He holds up his hand until the doors close a second later. We're alone.

I glance at him like he's lost his mind. Sean grins wickedly and reaches past me. He pulls the stop button and the elevator goes dark. Sean presses into me and my back slams into the wall. Sean's hands run over my sides as he leans in, pinning me in place.

My breath catches in my throat. The darkness in the tiny room chokes me. Panic slide up my throat.

Sean whispers in my ear, "I'm sorry, but you seriously think you can tell me that you're wearing nothing beneath this skimpy little dress and not make me hard the instant you say it? Feel me, Avery. That's what you do to me." Sean tilts his hips and presses into my leg. I feel his hard length press against me from under the constraints of his slacks.

I'm breathing harder and faster than usual. I hate elevators. I can't breathe. The first time Sean stopped it, we started moving again two seconds later, but this terrifies me. Beads of sweat form on my face. I suck in a jagged breath, trying not to scream.

Sean has me pressed against the wall, which makes it worse. I can't see him. I can't move. Voice shaking, I plead, "Stop."

Sean drops my hands and before I know it, my palms are against his chest and I'm pushing him away. Sean steps back. I feel a vacuum of cold air fill his place. He must push the button back in, because the lights flicker on and we start moving again.

Nervously, I tuck my hair behind my ear. I wish I could shrink into the corner and disappear. My heart is still pounding like I'm going to die. Elevators are like big caskets. When they stop, it feels like there's no air. My heart nearly exploded. It's not sexy, it's terrifying. And then Sean pinned me. I gasp, thinking that I'm going to be sick.

Sean gazes at me with a strange look on his face. Desire still swims in his eyes. His affection for me doesn't diminish, the way I thought it would. After watching me for a second, Sean says, "I'm sorry. I didn't realize you are claustrophobic." His eyes are burning a hole in my face, demanding that I meet his gaze.

When I look up, I can't breathe. Sean is so intense, so attractive. He lures me in and I never had a chance. "I'm not," I lie. No one's realized this about me. I hate it that Sean does. I try to break the gaze, but I can't.

"Then what upset you?" When I don't answer he steps closer to me. "Was it the way I touched you?" I shake my head. I know where he's going with this.

Swallowing hard, I answer. "I just didn't expect it, that's all."

Sean nods and seems to accept that as my answer. It isn't until later that I found out that he didn't accept it at all.

CHAPTER 13

Sean unlocks the door to the penthouse. I follow him into the room. My heart still beats too fast, too hard. When Sean throws his keys onto the hallway table, he follows me into the room. Taking my hand, he leads me to the center of the room. Sean closes the space between us and presses his body against mine. He starts to sway slightly, like we're dancing. I wrap my arms around him and hold on loosely. His hands slip over the back of my dress. I feel his fingers cup my butt before finding the hem of the dress insanely close. Sean's hands smooth over the outside of my dress and he looks at me. I know he's aroused. I don't have to feel his pants, I can see it in his eyes.

My heart thumps in my chest when he looks at me like that. My entire body responds to him and prickles. I want to feel his hands slip over my skin.

Sean seems to read my mind. Without breaking eye contact, he slides his hands down my sides, feeling my little black dress. When he reaches the hem, his hands move under the fabric. He pulls me closer and slides his hands around back, feeling my bare ass. He responds instantly. I can feel his dick pressing into my belly. The sensation warms me in a way that makes my insides pulse. Why do I react to him? Can't I just let him fuck me and not care?

The thoughts vanish along with every other logical thing in my brain. Sean dips his head to my neck and finds the place that makes me weak. He presses our bodies together, still swaying his hips gently against mine. One hand is firmly holding my butt and squeezes hard while the other drifts around to the front. He lowers his hand between us and dips his fingers between my legs. The response is instant. I moan and fall into him. I can't stand when he does that to me, but Sean makes me remain where I am.

"I expect you to stand here and do what I say," his voice is deep, commanding. It makes me want to obey him. I shiver, wondering what he's going to ask. "Pull up your skirt."

I inch the fabric up until he tells me to stop. My bottom is revealed in all its naked glory. Sean's eyes darken and fill with a carnal gaze that makes me too hot. "Legs apart." I shift my feet. "More."

I move again and now they are shoulder's width apart. Sean kneels in front of me. He presses his face against the V in my legs, breathing in deeply. He stares at my pussy for a moment, like he's trying to control himself, but he fails. Sean dips his head and licks the seam of my lower lips. I nearly jump. "Stay still, Smith," he scolds me.

To make sure I don't move this time, Sean holds onto my hips. When he lowers his head and licks me, every inch of my body flares to life. I gasp as his tongue strokes my sensitive folds. A spark ignites somewhere in my core and I want more. I need more. I hate how he does this to me, but I let him. Sean detected the parts of me that respond the most. That spot on my neck, I didn't even know it was there. It's nearly all the way around on my back, but Sean found it. One kiss there makes me so weak and so turned on. It's hard to not want sex when he kisses me there.

And now, this sexy man is on his knees at my feet doing the most divine things to me. I can barely stand. One more sweep of his tongue and my knees buckle. Sean stands and takes me over to the bed. That's when things change. He removes his belt and binds my wrists together. He explains what he's doing, what he needs. "You're right. I didn't call Black to play house with someone. I need something. I want this." His breaths are jagged. My heart races faster. I let him tie my hands before I realize what he's saying. Looking in my eyes, he asks, "Tell me no now if you can't do this."

"I don't know what you're doing," I confess, feeling afraid and stupid. My heart slaps against my ribs so fast that I think I'm going to stroke out.

Sean's eyes are so dark. Whatever he held back the last few times he was with me is coming forward. "I want to tie you down and have my way with you. I want you at my mercy. I want you to fight back."

I look into his eyes. I don't understand. "You want to rape me?" That can't be what he means, but after I say it, I see the look on his face. I know it's what he wants. My heart pounds harder, faster. "Sean—"

"Say no or yes. Nothing else. You asked what I wanted. This is what I want." His eyes penetrate me. There's a desperation in them. It tells me that he's barely in control of himself. I nod slowly. Tension lines Sean's neck. His hands tighten into fists. "Say it. I have to hear you say yes. I don't want to hurt you, but I might. Sex is power. I need to feel that right now. Avery," he breathes my name like he can't imagine taking another breath if I say no, "tell me what you want."

Sex is power. He needs to feel like he has some control over his life. I look down at my hands knowing how this is going to make me feel. I hate being pinned down. If he ties me up, I'll scream, but that's what he wants—complete power over another person. He's so fucked up.

And so am I, because I say, "Yes."

I don't have to say the word twice. Sean grabs me and throws me down on the bed. I try to roll away, but can't. Sean stretches my tethered hands above my head, straddling me as he moves across my body. Fear pulses through me. I can't move. I can't breathe. He reaches over the side of the bed and grabs something—a rope—and ties my hands down. I know he can't stop and I don't want to make him, but I'm scared. I don't know why. He's made love to me several times. *This is not love.* It was never love.

I twist and kick out at him. Sean grabs each foot and ties them to each bed post so that my legs are splayed. I'm face down with my butt hanging over the side of the bed. Sean moves slowly toward me. I want to tell him to stop. I want him to stop and say he loves me. I want something besides this, but this is what I offered.

Sean's hands tug up the dress, revealing my naked bottom. Without warning, Sean thrusts into me. I cry out, not ready for it. I can't move. I can't do anything. Sean pushes in hard at first, gripping my hips and pushing frantically. After a few minutes, maybe more, he slows down. I'm not wet enough. What he does hurts. I whimper even though I try not to make a sound. Sean stills. It doesn't feel good. Having him inside me doesn't feel like anything. He pulls out slowly. I want to scream.

This is what it's going to feel like with the other clients. I press my eyes closed, waiting to feel Sean pushing into me again, but I don't. Opening my eyes, I look for him, but can't see him. I hear his jagged breathing somewhere behind me.

A tear escapes from my eye and rolls down my cheek. I feel his eyes on my face. I know he sees it. My stomach clenches tight. I close my eyes willing my tears away. No more fall. No more will come. It doesn't matter what he does to me.

But Sean doesn't touch me again. I hear him sit down hard behind me. I struggle with the ties, hoping to free myself, but I can't. Before I realize what's happening, Sean's there and he unties me. I watch his face as he unties his belt from my wrists. He won't look at me.

I stand and rub my wrists and fix my dress. My heart is pounding. "You didn't have to stop."

"It felt wrong," is his only reply. Sean sits in a chair and hides his face from me. The way he leans forward, placing his elbows on his knees and resting his forehead on his hands makes it impossible to see him.

"Why?" I know I shouldn't ask that question, but I do.

Sean looks up at me with such sorrow in his eyes. He doesn't answer me. Instead he tells me more things that I don't want to hear. "Before, when we were in that elevator, when you made that noise—I knew you were afraid. I sensed it. It turned me on faster than anything else. You know why I don't want to do this right now? Because it's not enough, it's not pushing you all the way into your darkest fears. Tiny space with no light terrifies you. All I can think about is fucking you in there, making you so frightened that you scream while I fill you with come." Sean's breathing hard, like the idea is too appealing to resist. My heart beats harder, faster. "I was like you, once. I felt things by touching and tasting, but not now. I can do those things, but I crave the other so much more. We're a bad match, Avery. I'll break what's left of you. There's very little holding you together. I don't want to be the guy that turns you into this." He presses his fingers to his chest.

I'm stunned. I don't know what to say. Fear surges through me. I want to run, but I need to stay. "So, you need to hurt me to get off?"

Sean shakes his head after a moment. "No. I need to feel your heart racing and feel you trembling. It's the fear. I need your fear." Sean doesn't look at me. His confession weighs on his shoulders like he can't stand.

I don't know what to think of him or his needs. I can't fathom his life or this. The only thing I can think to say is the thought that keeps popping up in my mind. "But I'm afraid of you anyway." Sean's eyes cut to mine. I feel the world shift.

The words that I'm never supposed to say come pouring out of my mouth in a flood too fast to stop. "It doesn't matter what you do or what you say, I'm desperately afraid of you, Sean. Everything about you seems to bring me back to life. Your voice, your words, your face...I can't think when you're there and when you're gone, it's worse.

"When I saw you this morning, I was torn apart. I'd found your note, the one in your pocket. I thought you were cheating, that you had a wife and a baby. When you showed me her grave, I almost wished you were cheating. I could have walked away from that, but not from this. And that's what frightens me more than a dark elevator or a tiny closet." I hold my breath and try to stop the flow of words, but they don't stop.

I step toward him, almost afraid to touch him. The moment feels so brittle, like it could snap. "You evoke things in me that I've never felt, that I never thought I'd feel. And that's just it—I feel around you, and it's amazing. I've been numb for so long, wishing that I could seal off the pain that's seeping into my soul. Then you came along and I fell for you. I love you, Sean. I can't help it. And it terrifies me." Wide-eyed with a pounding pulse, I watch him react to my words.

Sean's eyes lock with mine, but he says nothing. He just looks at me. It's the worst thing he could possibly have done. A moment later, he turns and pinches the bridge of his nose. Sean doesn't look at me when he says it. "I'm going to tell Black to send me a different girl. You can go." His words feel like a knife to my gut.

I stare at him with a million thoughts racing through my mind. *He doesn't love me.* The thought beats me down into a bloody pulp. I can't stand to look at him. Saying nothing, I cross the room and grab my purse. I take the stack of bills that Miss Black gave me. I don't think about it. I just act on my feelings. This whole fucking charade can stop. I don't want his money. I don't want him. I want every trace of his existence scrubbed clean from my life. Anger builds inside of me. I need this money, but I need my sanity more. I fling the stack of bills across the room. The money flutters through the room like a gust of oversized snowflakes. Before Sean looks up, I'm gone.

My eyes sting horribly, but I won't cry. I take the elevator to the lobby. He doesn't come after me, chasing me like this is a movie. No, Sean is calling Black now, telling her that he wants someone else. I leave the hotel grounds, not concerned about my bracelet. Nothing can protect me from this. I obliterated what was left of my heart. I feel it dying inside my chest.

I stand at the curb for a second, too hurt to think. The limo isn't here. I'm freezing in this tiny little dress with no coat. I know that feeling, but now instead of providing comfort, it makes me feel sick. I walk, not going anywhere in particular. I pass people on the sidewalks and wish that I was someone else. I have nothing. No one. I spilled my heart, telling Sean exactly how I felt and he returned me. My cell rings a moment later. It's Black. I don't answer. I walk on, going nowhere, thinking nothing.

The frigid air numbs my skin and I welcome it into my heart. The numbness over takes me, and I hope that I never feel anything ever again.

THE ARRANGEMENT SERIES

This story unfolds over the course of multiple short novels. Each one follows the continuing story of Avery Stanz and Sean Ferro.

To ensure you don't miss the next installment, text **AWESOMEBOOKS** to **22828** and you will get an email reminder on release day.

MORE BOOKS BY H.M. WARD

DAMAGED

DAMAGED 2

SCANDALOUS

SCANDALOUS 2

SECRETS

THE SECRET LIFE OF
TRYSTAN SCOTT

And more.

To see a full book list, please visit:

www.SexyAwesomeBooks.com/books.htm

CAN'T WAIT FOR H.M WARD'S NEXT STEAMY BOOK?

Let her know by leaving stars and telling her what you liked about THE ARRANGEMENT VOL. 3 in a review!

CPSIA information can be obtained at www.ICGtesting.com
Printed in the USA
LVOW12s1624210115

423771LV00001B/83/P